KAY THOMPSON'S ELOISE

Eloise's Mother's Day Surprise

STORY BY **Lisa McClatchy**

ILLUSTRATED BY **Tammie Lyon**

Ready-to-Read

Aladdin

NEW YORK · LONDON · TORONTO · SYDNEY

ALADDIN PAPERBACKS
An imprint of Simon & Schuster Children's Publishing Division
1230 Avenue of the Americas, New York, NY 10020
Copyright © 2009 by the Estate of Kay Thompson
"Eloise" and related marks are trademarks of the Estate of Kay Thompson.
All rights reserved, including the right of reproduction in whole or in part in any form.
ALADDIN PAPERBACKS and related logo and READY-TO-READ are
registered trademarks of Simon & Schuster, Inc.
The text of this book was set in Century Old Style.
Manufactured in the United States of America
First Aladdin Paperbacks edition March 2009
2 4 6 8 10 9 7 5 3 1
Library of Congress Cataloging-in-Publication Data
McClatchy, Lisa.
Eloise's Mother's Day surprise / story by Lisa McClatchy ;
illustrated by Tammie Lyon.—1st Aladdin Paperbacks ed.
p. cm. — (Kay Thompson's Eloise) (Ready-to-read)
"Artwork in the style of Hilary Knight"—T.p. verso.
Summary: Nanny takes Eloise shopping for the "best best best" Mother's Day gifts.
ISBN-13: 978-1-4169-7889-3
ISBN-10: 1-4169-7889-5
[1. Shopping—Fiction. 2. Gifts—Fiction. 3. Mother's Day—Fiction.
4. Plaza Hotel (New York, N.Y.)—Fiction. 5. Hotels, motels, etc.—Fiction.
6. New York (N.Y.)—Fiction.]
I. Lyon, Tammie, ill. II. Thompson, Kay, 1909–1998. III. Title.
PZ7.M47841375Elf 2009
[E]—dc22
2008049718

I am Eloise.
I am six.

I live in the Plaza Hotel
on the tippy-top floor.

It is spring.
Time for sunshine.
Time for flowers.

Time for mothers.

Nanny says we must, must, must go shopping today. It is almost Mother's Day!

This is my dog.
His name is Weenie.

Weenie always goes
shopping with me.

We put on our sunglasses.

We put on our
springtime best.

Nanny says, "Do not forget your spring hat and your purse, Eloise!"

Oh, I love, love, love
to shop!

Nanny lets me
decide what to buy.
"First, we shall have
to buy chocolates," I say.

Weenie and I love chocolate.
So does Mother.

Nanny takes me
to Godiva.

Mother must have
the best, best, best!

"Next, we buy flowers,"
  I say to Nanny.
"This vendor will do!"

I pick the reddest roses
because Mother must have
the best, best, best!

"Now we shall buy her
a ring," I declare.

"Only Tiffany will do,"
I tell Nanny.
Mother must have the
best, best, best!

Only Saks Fifth Avenue will do. Mother must have the best, best, best!

Nanny, Weenie, and I
take our presents back
to the Plaza.

We hand them to the
manager to send them
to Mother.

"Wait, Nanny," I say
when we are done.

"I have one last thing."

"A box of chocolates for you.
And a rose."

Oh, I love, love, love, love Mother's Day!